LUCA LEARNS TO SWIM

"A Family's Swim Lesson Companion"

Barry Shrewsbury

with illustrations by

Kat Drayton

AuthorHouse™
1663 Liberty Drive, Suite 200
Bloomington, IN 47403
www.authorhouse.com
Phone: 1-800-839-8640

First published by AuthorHouse 12/10/2007

ISBN: 978-1-4343-0715-6 (sc)

Library of Congress Control Number: 2007903033

Printed in the United States of America
Bloomington, Indiana

This book is printed on acid-free paper.

authorHOUSE®

This book was a labor of love for me and wouldn't have been possible without the support and guidance of the following people:

My parents for their long standing belief in me
and their excellent editing skills
Ian T. for his part in making this book what it is
Marianne for her support and inspiration
Ron for arriving in the nick of time
Nina, you know why! - I Love You
Ian D. , Jessica and, of course, Luca

and

All my swim lesson families
for giving me the opportunity and joy of
working with and learning from their amazing children.

<u>Note to Parent Readers</u>
This book is meant to be an aid in *your* encouraging your child's learning process. It is not a substitute for developing a direct and personal relationship with a swim instructor in your home area.
Best Wishes For Your and Your Child's Success!

**NEVER ALLOW YOUR CHILD TO SWIM ALONE OR UNSUPERVISED AROUND, NEAR, OR IN A POOL OR OPEN WATER!
(EVEN "POOL SAFE" CHILDREN NEED SUPERVISION)**

For More Information:
curiousdolphin.com
lucalearnstoswim.com

Every year,
   youngsters all over the world
      begin the exciting adventure
         of learning how to swim.

This is the story
   of one of those children,
      a boy named...

Luca

Luca **loved** being in water.
He **loved** splashing and playing around in the shallow areas.

Luca also spent a lot of time watching his older brothers
as they swam and played in the deep end. It looked like so
much fun! Luca wondered if he would ever join them.
You see, he hadn't yet learned how to swim.

One day, he promised himself,
*I'm going to be able to swim
just like them!*

Then, one night, at the dinner table, Luca's father said, "Luca, guess what? We have some great news. We signed you up for swim lessons and you start tomorrow!"

Luca became so excited that he dropped his fork. He thought, *Boy! I'm finally going to learn how to swim.* He also began to feel a little worried. *What if it is too hard and I can't do it?*

Luca's parents noticed that he looked a little scared, so his dad said to him, "I can see you're nervous, and you know what? That's normal. Almost everyone feels that way when they start something new. All your brothers were nervous at first and look what great swimmers they are now. We know you will do well. Besides, it will be a lot of fun!"

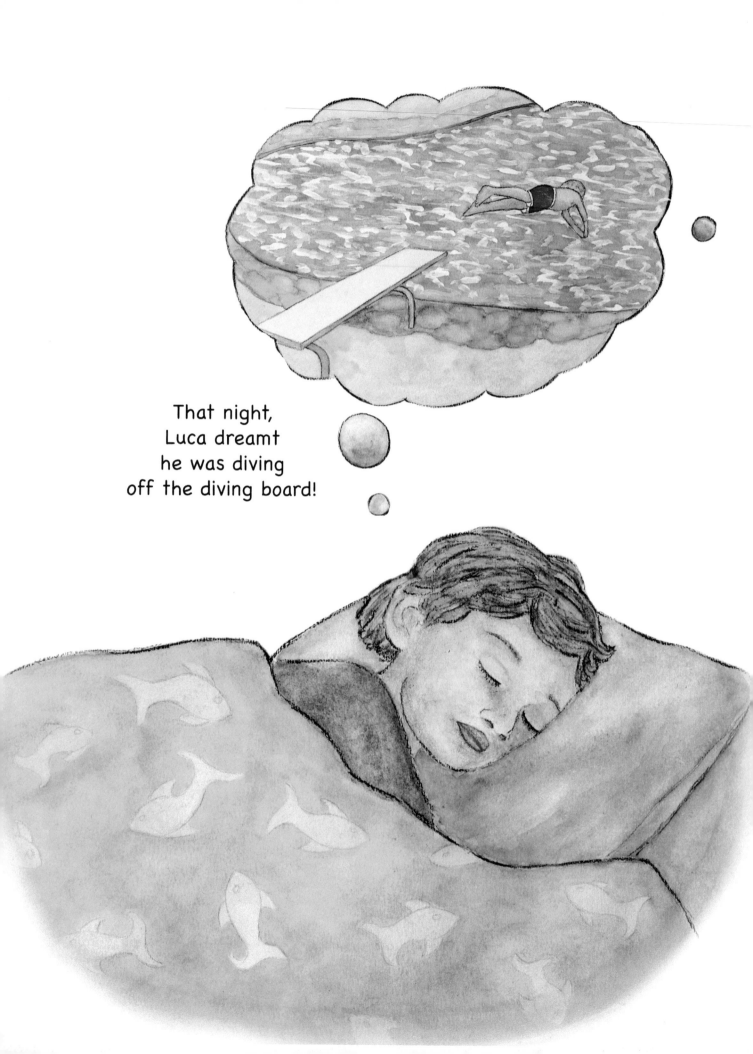

That night,
Luca dreamt
he was diving
off the diving board!

He dreamt he was picking up toys from the bottom of the pool!

He dreamt he was playing with his brothers in the deep end!
When he woke up the next morning, he was so excited
he could hardly wait for his lessons to begin.

While driving to the pool, although Luca looked excited, his mom could see he was a bit uneasy as well, so she told Luca some funny stories about his brothers' first swim lessons. She reminded Luca of when his oldest brother, Charlie, was so nervous that he put his swimsuit on inside out and backwards. This made Luca laugh, and before he knew it they had arrived at the pool.

Luca and his mom walked into the swimming area for his first lesson. He stopped, took a long look across the water and thought...

Wow, that pool is HUGE!
I don't think I'll ever be able to swim across it!

After Luca changed into his swimsuit, he and his mom sat down in the bleachers to wait for his lesson to begin. He noticed other children around the pool taking lessons and wondered what he was going to be asked to do that day.

Just then, a young lady with a big smile walked up, knelt next to Luca, and said, "Hi Luca! My name is Angela. I'm your instructor. Let's go to the steps in the shallow end so we can get started."

Luca liked her right away and smiled back as bravely as he could.

Angela took Luca gently by the hand and they walked to the edge of the pool to sit down and talk.

She said, "You know, Luca, it's fantastic that you want to learn to swim. However, before we begin, I must ask you to do one thing for me."

"What?" Luca asked curiously.

"Will you promise me that you'll do your best during the lesson? That is how you will learn to swim."

"Okay," answered Luca. Angela could tell that he was ready to become a swimmer, so they stepped into the pool to begin his first lesson.

First, Angela asked Luca to blow some bubbles in the water.
He did that with ease. "Great!" she said.

Next Angela asked Luca to put his face in the water
and he was able to do that too.

"Good job!" she cheered. "Now see if you can bend your knees and put your whole head underwater." Soon Luca was doing that easily as well. Angela said, "I can see you really do want to learn how to swim. Now, let's try something new."

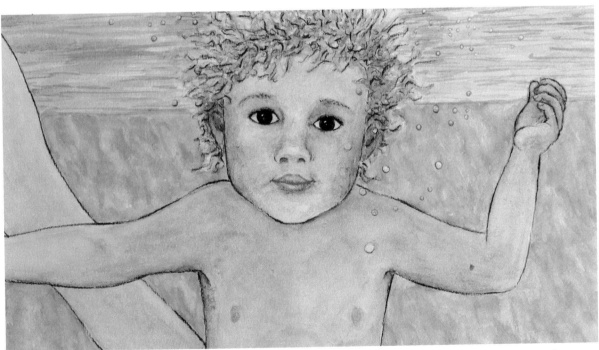

Angela asked Luca to put his head back under the water and this time to open his eyes. It took a few tries, but the last time he came back up he had a huge smile on his face and proudly told Angela, **"That was easy."**

Then Angela took some diving toys and placed them on the steps. "Now," she said, "Show me all you've learned. Put your head under the water, open your eyes, bend your knees, and pick up the toys one at a time." When Luca came up with the last toy in his hand he was grinning from ear to ear. **"That was really FUN! Can I do that again?"** "You bet!" Angela replied. And he did.

Finally, Angela and Luca took a dip under the water while she gently held him. Luca thought it was funny looking at Angela's face through the bubbles. When they came back up, his first lesson was over.

Luca could not believe how much fun he was having. Angela could see how proud Luca was, so she invited his mom to join them and see the new skills he had learned that day. Then, with Angela's help and encouragement, Luca showed his mom everything he had done. "Wow! I am so proud of you, Luca," his mom said, as she lovingly wrapped him up in his towel when he stepped out of the pool.

Luca was now well on his way to becoming a swimmer just like his brothers, but he still had a few more skills to learn before he would be **pool safe** and able to swim well.

Over the next few weeks, Luca and his mom went for several more lessons. Each time, Angela would have Luca begin by repeating the skills he had already learned. Then she would teach him a few new ones.

By the time he reached his last lesson, Luca had learned so much!

Luca could float and glide along the surface of the pool with his face in the water.

He floated on his back with confidence.

He would eagerly jump into the deep end, tread water, and swim back to the side **ALL BY HIMSELF!**

He could swim underwater and pick-up toys from the bottom of the pool, just like he had dreamed.

He could swim using his arms and legs at the same time.

He learned how to breathe while swimming longer distances.

Finally, with all the confidence and skill he had gained, Luca was able to swim from one side of the pool to the other! This made Luca happiest of all.

"I can swim now just like my brothers can!" he shouted to his mom.

"Yes, you can," exclaimed his mom. "We are all so proud of you. We knew you could do it! Now we know you are **pool safe** too."

After climbing out of the pool, Luca gave Angela a huge hug and said goodbye. Then, as he and his mom were walking to the car, Luca stopped and took one final look across the water and thought, *that pool wasn't so big and scary after all!*

THE END

Swim Lesson Considerations

These ideas and suggestions originated from my years of experience in answering parents' questions and observing what has worked best for my students' success.

1. Ask yourself what your goal is for your child. If you would like him to be able to swim, become pool safe, and retain skills, I recommend beginning formal lessons. If you would simply like to introduce him to water, a "Mommy and Me" class may be all you need.

2. If your child is fearful or anxious about learning to swim, I recommend private lessons. Your child will receive individualized attention, and, in the long run, you will probably feel it was worth the investment. Furthermore, her retention will be stronger with two or more lessons per week. If private lessons are unavailable, I recommend putting her in the smallest class available.

3. **Before lessons begin**: The entire experience will be made easier and more enjoyable for **everyone** if your child has become comfortable with putting her face in the water, with opening her eyes underwater, and with taking direction from other adults. These water skills can be introduced at home.

4. Arrive for the lesson early, have your child dressed and ready, and **always** have your child use the restroom before each lesson.

5. Many programs and instructors prefer the parent not be in view of their child during lesson time. This is especially important in the beginning when your child is adjusting to the process, and needs to be focused on the teacher and his instructions. Often you can find a viewpoint from which you can see without being seen.

6. Children differ in how long it takes them to transition from anxiety to growing self-confidence. Often children will be more resistant right before a breakthrough. Be patient! If you trust the process and allow your child to work through those fears, something magic happens. It is amazing to witness the transformation. If you feel things aren't going well, you might want to consider waiting another year. Trust your intuition! An additional year's maturity can make a huge difference in a child's ability to adapt to new experiences. You can use this year to work on developing the skills identified in consideration #3.

7. Read this book many times with your child before and throughout your child's lessons. This will help prepare you and your child for what to expect once the process begins. Because all the skills introduced in this book are ones your child will be asked to learn, reading this book together may lessen his fear of the unknown.

8. This will be one of the more memorable and rewarding experiences of your child's life. Enjoy it! You are providing him with some of the most important skills he will ever learn and something he will use and value the rest of his life!

9. Some organizations to contact regarding both private and group lessons are: the *Y.M.C.A., The Red Cross, and Swim America.** Also try your local pools, parks and recreation districts, health, golf and tennis clubs, and high schools. Look in the Yellow Pages under "Swim Schools." Ultimately, the best source is to ask fellow parents you respect for their recommendations.

* This is not an endorsement of the particular programs or organizations mentioned here.

NEVER ALLOW YOUR CHILD TO SWIM ALONE OR UNSUPERVISED AROUND, NEAR, OR IN A POOL OR OPEN WATER! (EVEN "POOL SAFE" CHILDREN NEED SUPERVISION)

Barry Shrewsbury

Barry has taught countless youngsters how to swim and enjoy the water, and especially, how to be *pool safe*. This story arises out of these experiences, the first in a planned series of children's books. Barry has long felt the need for a book which would support parents in their vital job of preparing their children for swim lessons.

Barry holds a Master's Degree in Athletic Counseling and has served as a middle school teacher in Los Angeles; a camp counselor and waterfront director; and a youth coach for swimming, water polo and baseball, in addition to his work as a swimming instructor. He resides with his wife and daughter in North Fork, California.

Kat Drayton

Born into an artistic family from New England, Kat now lives and works in Sedona, Arizona. She has worked with children for the past ten years and currently helps kids with special needs in the local school system.

Kat enjoys art projects that involve children. This is the second children's book she has illustrated.

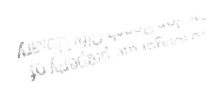

E   Shrewsbury, Barry
S
         Luca learns to swim

Printed in the United States
119. 1 LV00002B